中华优秀传统

文化故事

奉延旗　主　审
蔡虎志　胡翠娥　陈青扬　主　编
罗云涛　邓　旭　廖亮英　副主编

黑龙江科学技术出版社
HEILONGJIANG SCIENCE AND TECHNOLOGY PRESS

图书在版编目（CIP）数据

中华优秀传统文化故事：汉英对照 / 蔡虎志，胡翠娥，陈青扬主编；罗云涛，邓旭，廖亮英副主编 .

哈尔滨：黑龙江科学技术出版社，2024. 8. -- ISBN 978-7-5719-2559-8

Ⅰ . I247.81

中国国家版本馆 CIP 数据核字第 2024FN6423 号

中华优秀传统文化故事
ZHONGHUA YOUXIU CHUANTONG WENHUA GUSHI

奉延旗　主　审
蔡虎志　胡翠娥　陈青扬　主　编
罗云涛　邓　旭　廖亮英　副主编

出　　版　黑龙江科学技术出版社
地　　址　哈尔滨市南岗区公安街 70-2 号
邮　　编　150007
电　　话　（0451）53642106
网　　址　www.lkcbs.cn

责任编辑　赵雪莹
设计制作　深圳·弘艺文化　HONGYI CULTURE

印　　刷　三河市金兆印刷装订有限公司
发　　行　全国新华书店
开　　本　710 mm × 1000 mm　1 / 16
印　　张　4.25
字　　数　35 千字
版次印次　2024 年 8 月第 1 版　2024 年 8 月第 1 次印刷
书　　号　ISBN 978-7-5719-2559-8
定　　价　48.00 元

　　本书受到全国名老中医药专家陈新宇传承工作室建设项目（国中医药人教函〔2022〕75号）、湖南省发改委创新引导专项（湘发改投资2019-412号）、湖南省自然科学基金（2020JJ4474）、心病"四时调阳"重点研究室建设专项（湘中医药函〔2020〕51号）、"四时调阳"治未病湖南省工程研究中心（湘发改高技〔2020〕1006号）、湖南省科学技术厅重点领域研发计划（2019SK2321）、湖南省科技人才托举工程项目（2020TJ-N01）支持，特此致谢。

CONTENTS 目录

女娲补天

(Nüwa Patches Up the Sky)

　　远古时代，四根擎天大柱倾倒，九州大地裂毁，天不能覆盖大地，大地无法承载万物，大火不熄，洪水泛滥。在这种情况下，女娲冶炼五色石来修补苍天，砍断海中巨鳌的脚做撑起四方的天柱，用芦灰堆积起来堵住了洪水。天空被修补了，天地四方的柱子重新竖立了起来，洪水退去，中原大地恢复了平静，善良的百姓存活下来。

　　In ancient times, the four pillars that held up the sky collapsed and the earth cracked. The sky could not cover the earth, and the earth could not carry everything. The fire would not go out and the flood would not stop. In this case, Nüwa smelted five-color stones to repair the pillars of the sky. She cut off the feet of the giant turtle in the sea and used them as the pillars for supporting the sky. She also piled up reed ash to block the flood. The sky was repaired and the pillars for lifting the sky were erected again. The flood receded and calm was restored on the Central Plains. Kind-hearted people survived.

008

盘古开天地

(Pangu Split Chaos in the Sky and the Ground)

相传很久以前，天地未分，宇宙混沌。有个叫盘古的巨人，在这个混沌的宇宙之中沉睡了一万八千年。有一天，盘古突然醒了，见眼前一片漆黑，便用斧头朝黑暗猛劈过去，一声巨响后黑暗渐渐分散。缓缓上升的东西，变成了天；慢慢下降的东西，变成了地。天和地分开以后，盘古怕它们还会合在一起，便头顶天，脚蹬地。天在每天升高一丈，盘古也随着天越长越高。这样不知过了多少年，天和地逐渐成形了，盘古也累得倒下了。盘古倒下后，他的身体化作世间万物。他呼出的气息，变成了四季的风和云；他发出的声音，化作了隆隆的雷声；他的双眼，变成了太阳和月亮；他的四肢，变成了大地上的东、西、南、北四极；他的肌肤，变成了辽阔的大地；他的血液，变成了奔流不息的江河；他的汗，变成了滋润万物的雨露……

Legend has it that a long time ago, the universe was in chaos. There was a giant named Pangu who slept for 18,000 years in this chaotic universe. One day, Pangu woke up suddenly. Seeing the darkness in front of him, he slammed into the darkness with his axe. With a loud noise, the darkness gradually dispersed. Things that rose slowly became the sky and things that fell slowly became the earth. After the sky and the earth were separated, Pangu feared that they would still be together, so he pushed his head against the sky and kicked the ground. The sky rose by one foot every day, and Pangu also grew higher and higher as the sky grew. In this way, the sky and the earth gradually took shape. Pangu was so exhausted that he fell to the ground. After Pangu fell, his body turned into everything in the world. The breath he exhaled turned into the wind and clouds of the four seasons; the sound he made turned into rumbling thunder; his eyes became the sun and the moon; his limbs became the east, west, south and north poles on the earth; his skin became a vast land; his blood became the running rivers; his sweat become rain and dew that nourished all things...

大禹治水

(Dayu Combating the Waters)

帝尧时，中原洪水泛滥成灾，百姓苦不堪言。帝尧命令鲧治水，鲧在岸边设置河堤，可水却越涨越高，历时九年洪水仍未平息。后来，鲧的儿子禹继任治水之事。禹总结父亲治水失败的原因，以疏导河川为治水主导，利用水往低处流的自然趋势，疏通了河流。他和百姓风餐露宿，整天泡在泥水里疏通河道。他把平地的积水导入江河，再引入海洋。用时十三年，成功治理了中原的洪水。大禹因整治黄河水患有功，受舜禅让以继帝位。夏禹王登天子之位，并以自己的号封为国名，夏为天下之号，宣告夏王朝正式创建。

In Emperor Yao's time, floods in the Central Plains caused disasters, and the people were miserable. Emperor Yao ordered Gun to be in charge of taming the flood. Gun built dams, but the floodwater rose higher and higher, and nine years later, the flood had yet to subside. Later, Gun's son Yu continued to control the waters. Yu learned from his father's failure in water management, and adopted the method of channeling the water. Taking advantage of the natural tendency of water to flow down, he dredged the waterways. He along with others braved the wind and dew, stood hunger and slept in the open air. He was soaked in muddy water all day to create the channels that would eventually allow the floodwaters from the flat land into the river and then into the ocean. After 13 years of endeavors, the floods in the Central Plains were successfully conquered. Due to Yu's contributions in taming the Yellow River, Emperor Shun gine the throne to Yu. Yu the Great ascended the throne and declared the official founding of the Xia Dynasty with name of the city state assigned to him.

013

愚公移山

（Yugong and Two Mountains）

愚公移山的故事出自《列子·汤问》。相传冀州南部、河阳之北有太行、王屋二山。年近九旬的愚公在山北居住，苦于二山阻碍出行，便说服子孙挖山，邻居也来帮忙。其间有河曲智叟讥笑劝阻，而愚公均不为所动，以子孙无穷来反驳。最终感动天帝，天帝派天神将山挪走。

The story *Yugong and Two Mountains* is taken from *Liezi·Tangwen*. According to legend, there are Taihang and Wangwu mountains in the south of Jizhou and the north of Heyang. Yugong, who was nearly ninety years old, lived in the north of two mountains. The two mountains caused great inconvenience, so he persuaded his family's children and grandchildren to move the mountain. His neighbors also came to help. During this period, the wise old man Zhisou from Hequ ridiculed and discouraged Yugong, but he didn't stagger and argued by saying his infinite descendants could dig for generations. In the end, the Heaven God was moved and appointed another god to move the mountain away.

神农尝百草

(Shennong Tastes Hundreds of Herbs)

"民有疾，未知药石，神农氏始草木之滋，察其寒、温、平、热之性，辨其君、臣、佐、使之义，尝一日而遇七十毒，神而化之，遂作文书上以疗民族，而医道自此始矣。"神农最后因尝断肠草逝世，人们为了纪念他的恩德和功绩，奉他为药王神，并建药王庙，四时祭祀。

"People had disease and didn't know how to use herbs to cure disease. Thus, Shennong began to taste herbs. He observed the cold, warm, neutral and hot nature of each herb, and identified the composition and proportion of herbs. He once tasted seventy poisonous herbs in one day, but luckily the others found a kind of herb whose leaves helped detoxification. So the composition was recorded to heal the nation, and the history of medicine began from then on." Shennong finally passed away after tasting Duanchangcao, literally intestine−breaking grass. In order to commemorate his kindness and achievements, people regarded him as God of Chinese Medicine and built the medicine king temple for offering sacrifices.

玉兔捣药

(The Jade Rabbit Mashing Medicine)

　　玉兔捣药是中国神话传说故事之一，见于汉乐府《董逃行》。相传月亮上有一只兔子，浑身洁白如玉，被称作"玉兔"。白兔拿着玉杵，跪地捣药，做成蛤蟆丸，服用此药丸可以长生成仙。久而久之，玉兔便成为月亮的代名词了。

　　The story of *The Jade Rabbit Mashing Medicine* is one of Chinese myths, which is depicted in a Poems of Han Dynasty *Dong Tao Xing*. Legend has it that there was a rabbit on the moon. Since it was as white as jade, so it was called "Jade Rabbit". This white rabbit held the jade pestle, knelt down and pounded the medicine to make a toad pill. Anyone who took these pills would become immortal. Over time, the jade rabbit has become synonymous with the moon.

伏羲画八卦

(Fuxi Invents Eight Trigrams)

《易经》："古者包羲氏之王天下也，仰则观象于天，俯则观法于地，观鸟兽之文，与地之宜，近取诸身，远取诸物，于是始作八卦，以通神明之德，以类万物之情。"伏羲一画开天，打开了人们理性思维的闸门，解放了在疾苦中挣扎的人们。

The Book of *Changes* says: "In ancient times, Fuxi was the ruler of the world. He looked upward and contemplated the images in the heavens, and looked downward and contemplated the occurrences on earth. He examined the colors and patterns of birds and beasts that were suited to the environment. As to what was near he found things for consideration in his own person, and as to the remote in things in general. On this he devised the eight trigrams, to show fully the attributes of the spirit—like and intelligent, and to classify the qualities of the myriads of things." Bagua summarized everything between heaven and earth, enhanced people's rational thinking, and freed people from suffering.

夸父逐日

(Kuafu Chases the Sun)

　　"夸父与日逐走，入日；渴，欲得饮，饮于河、渭，河、渭不足，北饮大泽。未至，道渴而死。弃其杖，化为邓林。……"该神话故事出自《山海经·海外北经》，反映了中国古代先民战胜自然的愿望，现多用以比喻人矢志不移、坚持不懈、顽强拼搏。

　　"Kuafu raced against the sun, chasing after the sunset. He was thirsty and wanted to drink water. He drank water from the Yellow River and Weihe River. The water in the Yellow River and Weihe River was far from enough, so he went to drink water in the Great Northern Lakes. Before Kuafu arrived, he died of thirst halfway through, and the cane that he threw out with his last bit of strength before his death turned into a peach forest with luxuriant foliage and rich fruits." This mystical story is taken from the chapter called *Northern Lands Beyond the Seas* from the book *Classic of Mountains and Seas*, which reflects the desire of Chinese ancestors to conquer nature. It is now used as a metaphor for people's determination, perseverance and tenacious struggling.

精卫填海

(Jingwei Fills the Sea)

精卫填海，是中国上古神话传说之一。相传精卫本是炎帝神农氏的小女儿，名唤女娃。一日女娃到东海游玩，溺于水中。死后因内心不平，化作一种花脑袋、白嘴壳、红色爪子的神鸟，每天从山上衔来石头和草木，投入东海，然后发出"精卫、精卫"的悲鸣，好像在呼唤着自己。

Jingwei Fills the Sea is one of ancient Chinese myths. According to the legend, Jingwei was the youngest daughter of the Emperor Shennong, and her name was Nüwa. One day, Nüwa went to the eastern sea to play, but unfortunately drowned. After her death, the vengeful spirit turned into a bird which had a floral pattern on its head, white beak and red feet. Every day, it carried pebbles and twigs from the mountains and dropped them into the sea, and cried the plaintive wail of "Jingwei, Jingwei" as if calling itself.

后羿射日

（Houyi Shoots the Sun）

后羿射日，是中国古代神话传说之一。相传远古之时，大地出现了严重的旱灾，炎热覆盖了世界。原来，帝俊与羲和生的十个孩子都是太阳，他们住在东海扶桑树下，轮流出来在天空执勤，照耀大地。但有一天，他们因为任性，一起出现在天空，便给人类带来了灾难。为了拯救人类，后羿张弓搭箭，射下了其中九个太阳，只留下一个太阳，世代给予人类光明。

The story *Houyi Shoots the Sun* is one of ancient Chinese myths. According to the legend, in ancient times there was a severe drought on the earth and the heat scorched the world. It turned out that Dijun, an ancient Chinese emperor and Xihe, a solar goddess, gave birth to ten children. All of them were suns. They lived in Fusang tree in East Sea, and took turns to be on duty in the sky to shine their light through the earth. But one day, they appeared in the sky together because of their willfulness, which brought disaster to mankind. In order to save mankind, Houyi shot down nine suns and left only one sun to give mankind light from generation to generation.

028

沉香救母

(Chenxiang Saves His Mother)

沉香救母，是中国流传已久的神话故事。传说华山女仙"三圣母"思凡下界，婚配凡人刘彦昌，其兄二郎神大怒，施法将三圣母镇压于华山之下。三圣母之子刘沉香学得本领，大战母舅二郎神，最后劈开华山救得母亲，家人终得团聚。

The story *Chenxiang Saves His Mother* is a long standing Chinese myth. It is said that the goddess of Mount Hua named Sanshengmu longed for the life of the mortal world and married a mortal, Liu Yanchang. Her brother, Erlang Shen, a god, became furious and used magic to imprison Sanshengmu under Mount Hua. Chenxiang, the son of Sanshengmu, learned martial arts and fought against his uncle Erlang Shen. Chenxiang finally rescued his mother by cleaving through Mount Hua. The family was reunited at last.

黄帝战蚩尤

(Huangdi Defeats Chiyou)

黄帝战蚩尤，是中国上古神话传说之一。黄帝姬轩辕为统一华夏，使人民免于长期战乱，与九黎部落决战于涿鹿郊野。最后黄帝击败九黎部落，杀死了首领蚩尤。此后，华夏一统，各部族安居乐业，世人为感恩姬轩辕，尊称他为"黄帝"。黄帝的形象一直激励着无数优秀中华儿女奋发图强，为中华民族做出更多的贡献。

The story *Huangdi Defeats Chiyou* is one of the ancient Chinese myths. In order to unify China and save the people from years of war, Huangdi whose real name was said be Ji Xuanyuan fought against the Jiuli tribe in the Zhuolu county. Finally, Huangdi defeated the Jiuli tribe and killed its leader Chiyou. Since then, China has been unified and all tribes have lived and worked in peace and contentment. People in China are grateful to Ji Xuanyuan, who was honored as the Huangdi. The image of the Huangdi has always inspired countless outstanding Chinese people to work hard and make more contributions to the nation.

敦煌飞天

（Dunhuang Flying Apsaras）

　　敦煌飞天是在敦煌石窟中的壁画，它由印度文化、西域文化以及中华文明共同孕育而成。古代人们常常将飞天像画在石窟以及墓室的壁画上，象征着墓室主人的灵魂能羽化升天。在佛教尚未传入我国时，道教称其为"飞仙"，而随着后来佛教的传入和深入发展，慢慢改称其为"飞天"，而现在专指中国敦煌壁画艺术。

　　Dunhuang Flying Apsaras refer to a spiritual being painted in Dunhuang Grottoes. It was the hybrid of Indian culture, culture of Western Regions and Chinese civilization. In ancient times, people often painted Flying Apsaras on the murals of grottoes and tombs, symbolizing the soul of the owner of the tomb would rise to heaven. Before Buddhism was introduced into China, Taoism called it Feixian. With the introduction and spread of Buddhism, it was renamed Apsaras, and now it specifically refers to the art of Dunhuang murals in China.

夏至

(Summer Solstice)

每年的 6 月 21 日或 22 日，为夏至日。公元前7世纪，先人采用土圭测日影，就确定了夏至，此时太阳直射北回归线，是北半球一年中白昼最长的一天，且越往北白昼时间越长。夏至以后，太阳直射地面的位置逐渐南移，北半球的白昼日渐缩短。民间有"吃过夏至面，一天短一线"的说法。

June 21 or 22 of each year is the Summer Solstice. In the seventh century BC, our ancestors used Tugui to measure the shadow of the sun, determining the Summer Solstice. It is the time when the sun shines perpendicular on the Tropic of Cancer and it is the longest day of the year in the northern hemisphere. The farther north, the longer the hours of daylight. After the Summer Solstice, the sun's vertical overhead rays move toward their southernmost position, thus decreasing the daytime length in the northern hemisphere day by day. There is a folk saying that goes, "After eating noodles on Summer Solstice, daylight get shorter day by day."

冬至

（Winter Solstice）

冬至又名"一阳生"，意为阳气初生，是中国的第22个节气。早在2500多年前的春秋时代，古代先贤已经用土圭观测太阳测定出了冬至，它是中华民族24节气中最早制订出来的，时间在每年的12月21日~23日之间。冬至来了，雪花落了满眼，家中老人包着饺子，灯笼也悄悄挂起，年味越来越浓了。

The Winter Solstice, also known as "yiyangsheng", meaning the birth of Yang energy, is the 22nd solar term of the 24 traditional Chinese solar terms. As early as the Spring and Autumn Period, ancient sages affirmed the Winter Solstice by applying the instrument called Tugui for measuring the length of the sun shadow. It was the earliest solar term determined among the 24 solar terms of the Chinese nation. It falls between December 21 and 23 every year. As the Winter Solstice comes, a blanket of snow will cover the landscape. Elder people make dumplings and lanterns are hung outside the doors. The festive atmosphere grows stronger.

剪纸

(Paper Cutting)

剪纸是最古老的中国民间艺术之一，作为一种镂空艺术，它能给人视觉上以透空的感觉和艺术享受。剪纸用剪刀将纸剪成各种各样的图案，如窗花、门笺、墙花、顶棚花、灯花等。每逢过节或新婚喜庆，人们便将美丽鲜艳的剪纸贴在家中窗户、墙壁、门和灯笼上，节日的气氛也因此被烘托得更加热烈。

Paper cutting is one of the oldest Chinese folk arts. As a kind of hollow-out art, it can give the eye a hollow-out and artistic enjoyment. Paper cutting uses scissors to cut the paper into various patterns, such as window flowers, door paper cuts, wall flowers, ceiling flowers, lantern flowers, etc. During festivals or wedding celebrations, people paste beautiful and bright paper cuts on windows, walls, doors and lanterns at home, which make the festive atmosphere more intense.

040

京剧
(Beijing Opera)

京剧与越剧、评剧、豫剧、黄梅戏并称为中国五大戏曲剧种，被誉为中国国粹。京剧有多种不同的流派和唱腔，京剧场景布置注重写意，腔调以西皮、二黄为主，用胡琴和锣鼓等伴奏，同时又接受了昆曲、秦腔的部分剧目、曲调和表演方法，吸收地方民间曲调，是通过不断的交流、融合的结晶，是中国和世界的非物质文化遗产。

Beijing Opera, together with Yueju Opera, Pingju Opera, He'nan Opera and Huangmei Opera, is known as the five major operas in China. It is the quintessence of Chinese culture. Beijing Opera has many different genres and singing styles. The stage setup of Beijing Opera emphasizes freehand style and there are two main melody types—the xipi and erhuang. Accompanied by huqins, gongs and drums, accepted part of repertoire, tunes and performing methods of Kun Opera and Qin Opera. Meanwhile, it absorbs folk tunes in some regions. It is the crystallization of continuous exchange and integration and the intangible cultural heritage of China and the world.

中国功夫

（Chinese Kungfu）

中国功夫，是以技击为主要内容，以套路和搏斗为运动形式，注重内外兼修的中国传统体育项目。中国功夫讲究刚柔并济、内外兼修，是中国人民长期积累起来的宝贵文化遗产，是世界上独一无二的"武文化"，其衍生出的少林、咏春、太极等中国功夫在全世界广泛传播。

Chinese Kungfu, a traditional Chinese sport, is a series of fighting skills with movement sets and boxing styles as its form. Chinese Kungfu stresses the combination of hardness and softness, and cultivation of one's spirit and body. It is a precious cultural heritage accumulated by the Chinese people for a long time and evolves into a unique culture of martial arts in the world. Different styles of Chinese Kungfu such as Shaolin, Wing Chun and Tai Chi are widely spread all over the world.

044

中药

（Traditional Chinese Medicine）

　　中药又可叫作"本草"，我国最早的药物学专著就叫《神农本草经》，传说是由神农日尝百草所记录的。在我国，很多地区都有用中药材做作料来煲汤的习俗，"药食养生"的观念深扎于民间。一碗浓浓的中药汤，是寒热温凉不同药性的交融，是辛、苦、甘、酸、咸不同药味的调和，是水与火的淬炼和沉淀。

Traditional Chinese Medicine can also be called "materia medica". The earliest medicinal monograph in China is called *Shennong Ben Cao Jing (The Divine Farmer's Classic of Materia Medica)*, which is said to be the work by Shennong who tasted hundreds of herbs every day. In our country, many regions have the tradition of using Chinese herbs as condiments for making soup. The concept of "food and medicine stem from the same source" is deeply rooted among the folk. A bowl of thick traditional Chinese medicine decoction is the blend of Chinese medicines of cold, heat, warm and cold properties. The equilibrum of different medicinal flavors of spiciness, sweetness, sourness and saltiness, and the refinement through the combined force of water and fire.

书法

(Chinese Calligraphy)

　　书法是书写汉字的艺术。早在殷商时期，我国就有甲骨文出现，这种古老的文字已包含了书法的基本要素。汉字是一种象形文字，原本只是用来取代结绳记事的方法。后来，古代中国人通过聪明智慧逐渐创造出了各种字体，并将对汉字的书写艺术提升高度。好的书法就像一幅山水画，展现了汉字的艺术美。

　　Calligraphy is the art of writing Chinese characters. As early as the Yin and Shang Dynasties, oracle bone inscriptions appeared in our country. This ancient character already showed the basic elements of calligraphy. Chinese characters are hieroglyphics that were originally used only as an alternative to tying knots for recording events. Later, the ancient Chinese gradually created various typefaces with their wisdom and raised the writing of Chinese characters to the level of art. A good piece of calligraphy is like a landscape painting, showing the artistic beauty of Chinese characters.

048

陶瓷

（Ceramic）

中国是"陶瓷的故乡"。在英文中，"china"既有中国的意思，又有陶瓷的意思，可见陶瓷作为中国形象之一在世界的影响之大。我国制陶技艺的产生可追溯到公元前4500年至前2500年，它是我国古代劳动人民勤劳智慧的结晶。陶瓷与我们的日常生活息息相关，瓷碗、瓷盘、陶缸等陶瓷用品仍是我们寻常百姓不可或缺的生活用品。一件精美的陶瓷，饰以形形色色的花样图纹，兼具了实用价值和观赏美感。

China is the home of ceramics. In English, the word "china" can be used to refer to China as a country and also has the meaning of ceramics. It shows ceramics, one of the symbols of China, have a great influence in the world. The pot technology in China can be traced back to 4500 BC to 2500 BC. It is the crystallization of the diligence and wisdom of the ancient Chinese working people. Ceramics are closely related to our daily life. Ceramic bowls, plates, jars and other products are still indispensable in people's life. An exquisite ceramic piece decorated with various patterns has both practical value and aesthetic value.

四书五经

(The Four Books and Five Classics)

　　四书五经是我国古代重要的儒家经典著作。"四书"包括《论语》《孟子》《大学》《中庸》，"五经"包括《诗》《书》《礼》《易》《春秋》，其中贯穿了儒家以"仁爱"为核心的思想。孔子说："不学诗，无以言；不学礼，无以立。"四书五经是我们修身、立德、树人的根本。

　　The Four Books and Five Classics are important confucian classics in ancient times. The Four Books include The Analects of *Confucius*, *Mencius*, *The Great Learning* and *Doctrine of the Mean*, while the Five Classics include *Classic of Songs*, *Classic of Documents*, *Classic of Rites*, *Classic of Changes*, *Spring and Autumn Annals*. These classic works hold the confucian idea of benevolence as the core value. Confucius said, "If you do not learn poetry, you have nothing to say. Without an acquaintance with the rules of propriety, it is impossible for the character to be established." The Four Books and Five Classics play a vital role in strengthening morality and self cultivation.

051

中医医家

(Doctors of Traditional Chinese Medicine)

在中华民族五千年的岁月长河里，众多杰出的中医家以其精湛的医术守护了广大劳动人民的健康，从战国时期的扁鹊，到东汉时期的张仲景与华佗，魏晋时期的皇甫谧，明朝的李时珍……一味草药、一根银针、一张处方，中华大地孕育了独特的中医药学，中医药学亦守护中华大地。

In the five millennia of Chinese history, numerous outstanding doctors of TCM (Traditional Chinese Medicine) , such as Bian Que in the Warring States Period, *Zhang Zhongjing* and Hua Tuo in the East Han Dynasty, Huang Fumi in the Wei and Jin Dynasty, and Li Shizhen in the Ming Dynasty, have secured the health of laboring people with their superb medical expertise. The beautiful land of China is the home to TCM which utilizes herbs, silver needles and formula for treatment. TCM has and will safeguard Chinese people's health.

五岳

(Five Great Mountains of China)

五岳，是中华传统文化中五大名山的总称。分别为东岳泰山、南岳衡山、西岳华山、北岳恒山、中岳嵩山。五岳劈地摩天、气冠群伦，是古代民间山神崇敬、五行观念和帝王巡猎封禅相结合的产物。《周礼·春官·大宗伯》载："以血祭祭社稷、五祀、五岳。"自古山水为文人墨客所喜，千百年来，皇帝的祭祀仪式、僧侣的修行布道、雅士的赋诗作画，均为五岳留下了浓重的人文色彩。

The Five Great Mountains are the general name of the five famous mountains in Chinese traditional culture. They are Mount Tai (east), Mount Heng (south), Mount Hua (west), Mount Heng (north) and Mount Song (central) . The Great Five Mountains are famous for their high-rising peaks and magnificent landscapes. They are the product of ancient folk god reverence, the concept of the Five Elements and imperial excursions and meditation in ancient times. As *Zhouli · Chunguan · Dazongbo* records: "Blood sacrifice is offered to god of land, god of grain, five dieties, and mountain gods." Since ancient times, literati loved mountains and rivers. For thousands of years, the ancient emperors' sacrificial rites, monks' sermons, and scholars' poems and paintings all have left a strong humanistic touch for the Five Great Mountains.

五嶽獨尊

文以載道

觀

體

儒

藏

物

汉字

（Chinese Characters）

汉字，又称中文、中国字，属于表意文字，是汉语的记载符号，为世界上最古老的文字之一。千百年来，中华大地上历朝历代皆以汉字为官方文字。在信息交流尚不完善的古代，汉字维系了各地区的沟通，使辽阔版图的各族人民得以良好交流。现代汉字从甲骨文、金文、大篆、小篆，至隶书、草书、楷书、行书等演变而来，经过不断改进，汉字具备了更好的表意性，极大地促进了文化的发展与传播。

Hanzi, also known as Chinese or Chinese characters, belong to ideographic characters. They are recording symbols in Chinese and are one of the oldest characters in the world. For thousands of years, Chinese characters have been used as the official language in all dynasties in China. In ancient times, when information exchange was not convenient, Chinese characters facilitated communication among various regions and enabled people of all ethnic groups in the vast territory to communicate well. Modern Chinese characters evolved from oracle inscriptions on bronze, seal characters, small seal characters to clerical scripts, cursive scripts, regular scripts, running scripts and so on. With the continuous improvement, Chinese characters are more expressive, which greatly promotes the development and dissemination of culture.

民族风情

（Customs of Ethnic Groups）

在中国境内，共有56个民族。不同的民族有不同的文化习俗，饮食结构、服装特色、节日文化等均有不同，如蒙古族为游牧民族，以畜牧业为生，以牛、羊肉及奶食为主要食物；头饰是回族最典型、最富有特点的服饰，回族视白色为最洁净、最喜悦的颜色，回族男子多戴无檐小白帽；汉族的主要节日为农历的春节，为一年中家庭团圆的日子。中华各民族虽风情各异，却能团结统一、共同繁荣。

There are 56 ethnic groups in China. Different ethnic groups have different cultures and customs, which can be reflected in their dietary structures, clothing cultures and festival cultures. For example, Chinese Mongolians are nomadic people. They live on animal husbandry and take beef, mutton and dairy products as their staple food. As for the Hui ethnic group, the headwear is their most characteristic garment. They regard white as the cleanest and favourite color, and the Hui men typically wear small white caps without eaves. The most important festival for the Han nationality is the Spring Festival in Chinese lunar calendar, which is the time for family reunion in a year. Although different ethnic groups in China have different customs, they can unite to mutually prosper and grow.

诸子百家

（The Hundred Schools of Thought）

　　诸子百家是后世对华夏先秦学术思想人物和派别之总称。诸子是指中国先秦时期老子、庄子、孔子、孟子、荀子、墨子、列子、孙子、申子、韩非子、鬼谷子等学术思想代表人物。春秋后期已出现颇有社会影响的道家、儒家、墨家、名家、法家、兵家、阴阳家等不同学术流派，而至战国中期，百家争鸣，众多学说纷呈，丰富多彩，为中华文化奠定了深厚基础。

The Hundred Schools of Thought is the general term for the philosophers and schools of the Chinese Pre-Qin Period. "Zhuzi" refers to Lao Tzu, Chuang-Tzu, Confucius, Mencius, Xunzi, Mozi, Liezi, Sun Tzu, Shenzi, Han Feizi, Guiguzi and other representatives of academic thoughts during this period. In the late Spring and Autumn Period, Taoism, Confucianism, Mohism, Masters, Legalism, School of the Military, School of Yin-yang and other academic schools of great social influence emerged. In the mid-Warring States Period, hundreds of schools of thought contended and various theories flourished, which laid a solid foundation for Chinese culture.

中华美食

(Chinese Cuisine)

　　中国菜是中华文化的重要组成部分，既包括源自中国各地区的菜系，也包括来自海外华人的菜系。中国菜已经影响了亚洲的许多其他菜系，并根据当地口味进行了调整。中国菜的主要原料，如大米、酱油、面条、茶、辣椒油和豆腐。其主要餐具和厨具，如筷子和炒锅等，现在在世界各地都可以找到。

Chinese cuisine is an important part of Chinese culture. It includes cuisines originating from diverse regions of China as well as the cuisines from overseas Chinese. Chinese cuisine has influenced many other cuisines in Asia, with modifications made to cater to local palates. Chinese food staples such as rice, soy sauce, noodles, tea, chili oil, and tofu, and the tableware and cooking utensils like chopsticks and the wok, can now be found worldwide.

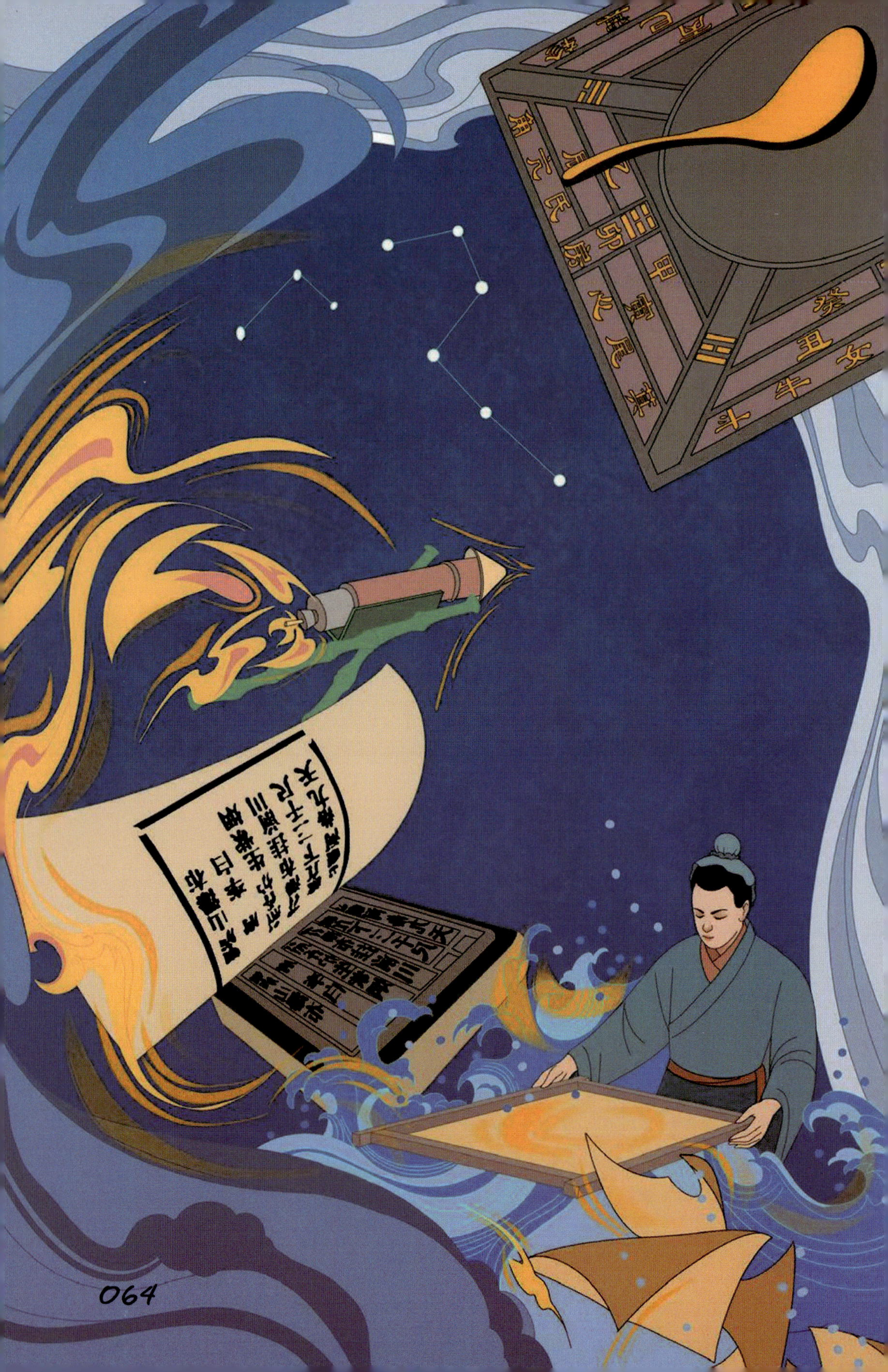

四大发明

(The Four Great Inventions)

四大发明是中国古代的发明，在中国文化中有着悠久的历史意义，是中国古代先进科学技术的象征。它们是指南针、火药、造纸术和印刷术。这四项发明对世界文明的发展产生了深远的影响。然而，一些现代中国学者认为，中国的其他发明可能更复杂，对中国文明有更大的影响——四大发明只是突出了东西方之间的技术互动。

The Four Great Inventions are inventions of ancient China. They are celebrated Chinese culture for their historical significance and serve as symbols of ancient China's advanced science and technology. The Four Great Inventions refer to the compass, gunpowder, papermaking and printing. These four inventions had a profound impact on the development of civilization throughout the world. However, some modern Chinese scholars have opined that other Chinese inventions were perhaps more sophisticated and had a greater impact on Chinese civilization while the Four Great Inventions serve merely to highlight the technological interaction between East and West.

长江黄河

(The Yangtze and the Yellow River)

　　长江是亚洲最长的河流，是世界上第三长的河流，也是世界上流经一个国家的最长河流。它发源于唐古拉山（青藏高原）的各拉丹冬峰，流经6300千米。它的流域占中国陆地面积的五分之一，居住着全国近三分之一的人口。黄河是中国第二长的河流，估计长度5464千米。它发源于中国西部青海省的巴颜喀拉山。长江和黄河在中国的历史、文化和经济中发挥了重要作用。

The Yangtze is the longest river in Asia, the third longest in the world. It is also the longest river in the world to flow entirely within one country. It rises at Mountain Geladaindong in the Tanggula Mountains (Tibetan Plateau) and flows 6,300 km. Its drainage covers one-fifth of the land area of China, and is home to nearly one-third of the country's population. The Yellow River is the second-longest river in China at the estimated 5, 464 km. It originates in the *Bayan Har* Mountains in Western China's Qinghai province. The Yangtze River and the Yellow River both play a significant role in the history, culture and economy of China.